T0164795

5 SENSES

LOVING A PERSON WITH ALL 5 SENSES

NICOLE ASBURY

COPYRIGHT © 2007 BY NICOLE ASBURY.

LIBRARY OF CONGRESS CONTROL NUMBER: 2007902214

ISBN: HARDCOVER 978-1-4257-6775-4

SOFTCOVER 978-1-4257-6759-4

All rights reserved. No part of this book may be reproduced or transmitted in any form or by any means, electronic or mechanical, including photocopying, recording, or by any information storage and retrieval system, without permission in writing from the copyright owner.

This is a work of fiction. Names, characters, places and incidents either are the product of the author's imagination or are used fictitiously, and any resemblance to any actual persons, living or dead, events, or locales is entirely coincidental.

This book was printed in the United States of America.

To order additional copies of this book, contact:
Xlibris Corporation
1-888-795-4274
www.Xlibris.com
Orders@Xlibris.com
38889

5 SENSES

CONTENTS

Acknowledgement 7
Prologue: Self-worth 9
Five Senses 11

Chapter 1:   Just Another Day 13
Chapter 2:   Spa Visit 15
Chapter 3:   Excitement 17
Chapter 4:   Dating 19
Chapter 5:   Could My Prayers Be a Reality? 21
Chapter 6:   Thoughts 22
Chapter 7:   Time 23
Chapter 8:   Breakdown 24
Chapter 9:   Chillin' 26
Chapter 10:   Trip 27
Chapter 11:   Paris 29
Chapter 12:   Wonderful 31
Chapter 13:   Partying 35
Chapter 14:   Catch-up Day 36
Chapter 15:   Sunday 37
Chapter 16:   You 40
Chapter 17:   A Wake-up Call 42
Chapter 18:   Hanging Out with the Girls 43
Chapter 19:   Engagement 45
Chapter 20:   Planning or Not? 48
Chapter 21:   Thinking 51
Chapter 22:   Uncertainty 52
Chapter 23:   Surprise 53

Epilogue 57

Acknowledgement

I will like to thank Lord for giving me a gift to write and express myself thru my writing. I will like to thank my parents for encouraging, supporting and understanding my dream. My brother "A" I am glad and blessed to have a brother like you. You are awesome! To the one that seen the struggle, trial and tribulation that made me strong my daughter "N" you are my heart and soul. I'm blessed to have a daughter that understood the long nights of writing and trying to make this dream a reality.

To my intermediate family thanks for your support.

To my girls Harmony, Chelsea, Nakeba, Jean & Debbie, thanks for keeping me lifted when I didn't know if I was coming or going. Ladies you are the best and one of a kind. Love you all!

To the woman that helped me out in the beginning with the editing of my book and giving me pointers. Thank you Regina Lawson-Abrams. I will see you soon with your editing business.

To the man that made it possible for the book cover Blac Pantha Production. Thank you for taking the time to put the sketch together and making my book come to life.

To my play brothers Kenny, James, Dorsey, Charles, Melvin & Reco thanks for giving me advice, support and encouragement and being a true friend.

My neighbors on Princeton you guys are wonderful and thanks for being real and sincere.

To everyone that believed and had faith in me thanks.

PROLOGUE

SELF-WORTH

Things I have experienced in dating. I have had a chance to sample every variety of men except the gay ones. I pray that I haven't come across any that are living the double life. I'm just glad I'm able to talk about it.

Well, I have dated the fast life; a drug dealer, a stripper, and an entertainer. It is fun for a minute, but no one has the time for love. Everyone is out chasing paper, and everyone is out chasing them. You can be about them, but they are all about themselves. So the best thing is to move on to the next person. They are wonderful lovers, but don't get me wrong, they lack something that I need, and I will tell you later about it.

I have dated the corporate type, the teachers, and the self-employed; it's about the same. Only difference is that you don't have to worry with the nonsense as much as mentioned previously. They are more attentive, but at times they can be overwhelming with their schedules and lifestyle. These types of men say they are ready for realness, but when you give it to them, they shy away. They can be arrogant, or even dominant, at times. They also lack something that I need, and I will tell you later.

I have dated the regular nine-to-five guys, the truck drivers, and just regular folks. They have and can have all the drama that was mentioned about the rest. Basically there's not much difference because at the end of the day, you have to decide if this is something you want or need. When you think you have something better, they are always screaming about life issues. We all have life issues; we have to deal with them accordingly. They lack something also.

If someone wants to be with you, there's nothing to keep them away from you. They will make every effort if they are being true. Never compromise your worth for no one. Don't give all you have to someone that's not willing to compromise with you. When you constantly compromise, then there's nothing left, and you lose sight of yourself. God gave you life to enjoy life and love living it. Do not waste it on someone that's not worth the air you breathe. So when someone comes into your life by paying your bills, sex, accepting your children, but then turns around and cheat, what's that? When you say you love someone, you love them completely. Don't play games when you know you don't know how to play. Keep it real. Just because you put your pants on like I do. Doesn't mean you can walk all over me. Go and sit down and reevaluate your life because you really haven't gotten it together. Our lives today seem like a roller coaster that will never end or never stop to let you off. It just keeps on going. We as people need to love and appreciate ourselves. Society has gotten us to accept things that are not true and shouldn't be accepted. I'm not knocking what you like, just be honest about it. We can save a lot of heartache and bloodshed if we just communicate and open our hearts to truth. Then you wonder, what is truth? Does it exist, or is it just something to say because it sounds good? If you can't love yourself, who do you think can love you?

Love isn't love until you have learned to love.

Five Senses

I wish I could take a journey back in time and look at my life all over again. I imagine what steps I would have taken to make myself a better person. But I wouldn't go back because that was the battle. Now I'm striving to do better because I have lived and am still living. No need to go back because this is what it is. I want to be loved the right way. I want the Lord to send him to me. I don't have time to raise someone else's son. So when you come, please be ready to walk with me, not run. Because I want to be able to enjoy you through the five senses. I want to be able to taste your love, I want to feel you, I want to hear everything you say, I want to smell you, and I want to see the love in your eyes. I want to be in love with all five senses.

Chapter 1

JUST ANOTHER DAY

It was like any other day, work as usual. It was busy at the spa after Christmas, and we were getting ready to bring in a new year in a couple of days. I needed a mental break because I was beginning to be overwhelmed by so many things that were taking place, and all of them were taking a toll on my body. I didn't have a personal life. Work consumed me, and of course, that left no outlet for a man. My girls and I would go out sometimes, but that was only once every blue moon. They were so engaged with their mates we hardly connected with each other aside from phone calls. And only if something was bad or very good. I had a partner in crime, but I haven't tried to call him. He calls me, but I don't have time to return the calls. I have been tied up with work and just haven't had the time to hang out. Since my "toy" is still working, I think I am good for a while.

It was a Friday night, around eight. I went to the grocery store to pick up some items because I wanted some tilapia and grits. I was looking at some fruit because I haven't had a good pineapple in a while. I was checking out the pineapples when I saw this man in the produce section that caught my eye. He was dressed in some beige wide-leg pants, and a button-down shirt with cuff links on and wearing wide camel toe shoes. I could smell his scent from where I was standing. I was getting light-headed because he had to be six feet or more with nice brown skin the color of chocolate. His hair was cut short and looked wavy, like they say about "good hair." He was a thick brother, probably 215 pounds solid (just guessing).

When he noticed I was looking (more like staring), he flashed this amazing smile. When he did that, I almost dropped the damn pineapple! I was completely caught up and had to come back to reality. I felt that poetic moment coming out. I went back to what I was doing because it was too much for me to take in. He came over and started looking at the pineapples, and he said, "It's hard to find a sweet pineapple these days."

I didn't reply because I was so nervous. He asked me if I was okay. I said yes, I was fine, I was just smelling the pineapple to see if it was a sweet one. I hurried up and picked my pineapple and left. I told him good luck in finding that sweet pineapple. I was like, *Damn, I should have struck up a conversation with him because he was inviting me to converse with him, but I didn't.* He smelled so damn good to me. I had to focus on what I was getting in the store. I was checking out the tilapia and salmon. I didn't know which one I wanted because both of them were looking delicious. I got both of them. I went by the magazine aisle, and I picked up *Sister2Sister* and *Essence*. I was looking at some of the hair magazines to see if I liked any of the new styles.

Suddenly I started smelling his scent. I knew my nose was not playing tricks on me. I wanted to turn around so quick, but I didn't. I heard someone say, "Smart and sexy." I turned around, and I said, "Excuse me." It was him again. This time I was able to look at him directly in the eye, and I thought I was going to pass out. He had those green or gray eyes, whatever their color was. I heard him say something, but I heard someone down the aisle sneeze, which broke my daze. I was saying to myself, *What in the hell is going on with me? This is what happens when you haven't seen a good-looking man in a while.*

He said something to me. I was like, "Okay." What in the world did I say okay to? He repeated what he said, thank God. He asked me if I was a seafood lover.

I said, "Yes, I am."

He said, "Forgive me, my name is Jamal."

"Nice to meet you, Jamal." I told him I had to go because I didn't want my fish to get too warm.

He said, "What is your name?"

"Sparkle," I answered.

"Sparkle?"

I said yes.

He just smiled. He asked if I would like to exchange numbers. He gave me his business card, and I gave him mine. He was saying his back was killing him.

I told him, "I bet. Call for an appointment."

"I will."

I said, "Have a good night."

"You too."

I walked away. I wanted turn around to see if he was watching, but I didn't. I checked out a love story movie from the local video store. Got home and took a long hot shower that was very relaxing. I went into the kitchen and cooked my tilapia and grits. So I ate my meal and watched the movie. The movie was getting good till I fell asleep. I woke around 3:00 a.m. and got into bed.

Chapter 2

SPA VISIT

The next morning I cleaned the house and went into the office. I was having a flashback about the encounter at the grocery store with Jamal. When I was in the office, one of my employees said, "I need for you to come up front."

Everyone knew I didn't have a man, and they couldn't remember me having one. They were trying to hook me up with clients, and clients were trying to hook themselves up with me. I didn't mix business with pleasure. Sometimes it was tempting, especially when it was one of your favorite entertainers trying to hit on you. I wasn't buying what they were selling because they had families. These men will never stop if you don't stop first.

I was asking Shanda, my receptionist, "Why do I need to come up front?"

She said, "We have a new client, and he wants to take a tour of the serenity wellness center."

I told her she could take him. She said he requested that I show him around.

I said, "Show him around."

Shanda was like, "He's fine and smells wonderful. What is the client's name? Mr. Princeton."

I went out to meet the client; it was Jamal. All I could do was smile, and when he smiled, my heart started beating fast. But I had to remain cool because I was at work, and I didn't want Shanda trying to figure anything out. I got back into my business mode. I showed him around the center. He was very impressed with the spa/salon. He said he heard about the center but never had time to stop by. I said I hope what he heard was all good. He said yes, it was. "Since I seen it I can understand its serenity." I said thanks. He asked who designed and decorated the place.

"You are looking at her," I said.

He said, "You have awesome taste."

I said thanks. We were getting close to the front.

He said, "I want to know if you would join me for dinner tonight if you are not busy."

I said it wouldn't be appropriate to mix business with pleasure.

He argued, "I didn't meet you at the spa, I met you at the grocery store. So we are not breaking the business-and-pleasure mix. Will it be okay if I called you?"

I said only if it was concerning an appointment. "I don't know about tonight because I'm trying take care of some things for Valentine's Day."

He made an appointment with me for next week. I said thank you for stopping by, and we shook hands and said good-bye.

Then came Shanda, being nosey as usual, but she's an awesome receptionist. She asked me what my expectation of Mr. Princeton was. I asked, expectation about what?

"Mr. Princeton, he's hot. Don't you think? He's handsome." Shanda was like, "You didn't get a number or asked out?"

I told her she needed to be doing her job and stop trying to be a dating game host. I went back into my office and started working. My cell phone started ringing and when I answered it, I was surprised. It was Mr. Princeton on the phone. I was thinking about him, and coincidence, it was him. He stated that since I didn't answer his question earlier, he would call me since I wouldn't be under the radar at work.

I was on the phone, blushing my behind off. If he could see it, he would be laughing at me.

Chapter 3

EXCITEMENT

Well, after speaking with Jamal, I was energetic, and I don't know what it was that got me thinking about him. I was so wide open that I finished majority of the mailing for Valentine's Day and whatever else that needed my attention. It was around six o'clock when Jamal called.

"Did I surprise you by calling again?" he asked.

I told him yes, I was surprised to hear from him again today. He wanted to know if I'd thought about having dinner with him tonight. I was a little hungry, so I agreed. He wanted to meet at Centennial Olympic Park and told me to park by the hotel. I was wondering what he had in store for the dinner date, but I let him do his thing. I pulled up to the place in my gray Lexus GS 430. Life had been good for me to have the nice things in life and still be humble. After parking, I was looking for Jamal. Jamal pulled up in a baby blue Mercedes S500 . . . beautiful. He parked, and he had a picnic basket, blanket, and some other goodies.

There was a very nice January-night breeze, and the sky was clear. We found a nice spot on the lawn and spread out the blanket. He was taking items out of the basket, which included a bottle of wine, wineglasses, music, items from the local market, and flowers. He poured the wine, and we toasted to our first date and many more to come. I had to raise my eyebrow to that one because I was just meeting this guy, and I didn't know what to expect, but I was going to go with the flow. He gave me flowers and a kiss on the cheek. I was getting warm because the kiss was soft but sensual. The food from the local market was divine, and he had some desserts. We shared the carrot cake together. We talked about what was going on in the world, our world. It was just a nice conversation between the two of us.

After eating, we slow-danced to mixed CD with slow jams. About that time, the sunset was gone, and a full moon took the place of the sun. Being in his arms was making me feel that I could really get use to this. We packed up our things and put them in his car, and he asked me if I wanted to take a walk around the park. I said yes, but that I needed to change my shoes because these heels were killing a sistah. He started laughing at me. I was glad I had my gym bag in the car still, and I changed my shoes.

We started our walk, talking, laughing, and holding hands. The night was coming to end. It was eleven o'clock on a work night, and we called it a night. He walked me to my car and gave me a hug and a kiss on the other cheek. He told me to have a safe trip home and to give him a call when I arrived safely. The night had turned out to be very romantic, and we had a lot in common. More than I thought. On the way home, I was replaying the events that took place, and I had this big smile inside and out. I looked over at the flowers. There were some tulips and some other type of flower. They were beautiful, and I noticed that there was a note or card with them. I wanted to read it, but I waited till I got home. The card was one of those humorous ones that made me laugh. As soon as I arrived home, I called him to let him know that I made it home and thanks for the card. We talked for a while and said our good nights. I slept like a baby that night.

Chapter 4

DATING

There were more dates and lots of time spent together. We finally decided that we were ready for a relationship. We had plans to go to Miami Beach for our Valentine weekend getaway, but we had to reschedule. We had to take the trip a week after because the spa was extremely busy. I had clients coming left and right. We left on a Thursday night because I was tired and so ready to be pampered. When we got to Miami, it was so alive. The hotel we were staying at was a five-star hotel, but I was ready to put my dancing shoes on. Even though I was tired, I was ready to let my hair down and have some fun with my man. I could tell he was feeling the same vibe I had because he was making suggestions himself.

We got into our rental car and decided to get something to eat and take it back to the room. We would eat, take our shower, and be out. That didn't happen. It was a beautiful night, and there was a nice breeze. We found a cozy restaurant and ate outside on the balcony, enjoying the view. It was going on 10:30 p.m. We were dressed, but when you get off a plane, you just need to take a shower sometime.

We ended up driving to a neo soul/poetry club that was located near the hotel. When we got there, it was so alive, the music was on point, and the poets were making you feel like you were in their writing. I just loved the ambience, the nice and relaxing atmosphere. We ordered drinks and were pretty happy after having had a couple. We didn't get back to the hotel until about 4:30 a.m. We took our showers and then went to sleep, knocked out from all the activities.

That next day, around noontime, we both got up and dressed. We turned our phones off when we got into bed that early morning. We knew how owning your business could be, and we didn't want to be disturbed. We missed breakfast, but we went out and had brunch. Then we both turned on our phones. We took an hour to take care of the messages. We decided to see the city. It was a warm, sunny day, no clouds whatsoever, just beautiful. I was glad he rented a convertible. It's cool when you're riding, but when you stop, your ass will burn up.

We went shopping because that's one of my favorite pastimes. He didn't mind the shopping because he liked to shop too. I was saying to myself that this might be a wonderful relationship but I got to stay focus. We found a bistro and had a late lunch, as it was going on 7:00 p.m. We decided to chill at the hotel that night. I said to myself, *A Friday night, but not alone.* At the hotel, they had a club there and restaurants too. So we were good for the evening.

We took our things back to the room, and he asked me if I wanted to take a walk on the beach. I was like, "Sure." We grabbed a towel and walked along the beach, laughing and playing. It was a warm night, there was a steady breeze off the ocean, and I was with my man. The night was so romantic, the sky had a full moon that cast an image on the ocean. As we were walking down the beach, Jamal turned to me. As we stood there face to face, I felt everything that he wanted to give me, and then he looked into my eyes and then slowly started kissing me. And then he slid his tongue into my mouth, and I accepted. The kiss was so intense that I felt light-headed. That's how passionate and deep it was.

Jamal's hand rubbed against my face and his other hand was moving slowly down the middle of my back. I felt the warmth of his hands, and it felt good as his hands roamed my body. He's cologne was so masculine, the kind that would stop you in the mall or the street and make your hormones start up. He was pulling me closer and closer till I could feel his breath on my neck. I was feeling his passion that he wanted to give, but I pulled away because I was not ready for all this the foreplay; kissing, and hugging was too much to bear. Even though we were sharing a room with double beds, I wanted him like a lion that hadn't eaten in days, and he was my beef . . . I wanted every bit of him. We walked back to the room with his arm around me, and I was saying we could wait.

We enjoyed the rest of the weekend with no pressure or worries. It ended up being a good weekend but also a weekend with my defense on high. Jamal wanted to know if he did anything wrong, I said no, he didn't. This was a gentleman, opening doors, rubbing my feet, and cooking his ass off, but most of all, he was a deep brother that could challenge me mentally. We could converse all night just about life and things that surround us. I had to let my guard down before I pushed this man away. It's been a while for me with dating, intimacy, and companionship. But right now let me get my shit together.

Chapter 5

COULD MY PRAYERS BE A REALITY?

Lord, send me a man that is right in your image. I know that no man is perfect besides you, but can I have one that has a pure heart that loves one and only one, can that be or not? I have been through too much to turn around, and now it's my turn to shine. I have shined for so many, but no one has shined for me. When I think I have found something, it has always been the opposite . . . more chaos.

Chapter 6

THOUGHTS

I'm sitting here and wondering about how in the world I ended up with these knucklehead men. Relationship after relationship, the same bullshit. Just when you think you have a rose, it ends up being a thorn in your side. No matter how hard you to try to take care of the rose, it seems to prick you every time to the point that you bleed.

I know my closet isn't clean, but these are my thoughts on things that bother me. Men and women are so similar but yet so different when it comes down to cheating. Do men cheat because they can? Do women do it because they need what they are not getting? Is this the reason why women go to women? Are they tired of men's bullshit, or is it the comfort level? Who the hell knows? So why would you want relationships with the same sex when you know both of you are emotional? Men on men, men on the down low, or just men who don't know what they want. If you are going to be bi, just let people know and let them decide if they want to be involved with the situation. If they don't want to be involved, you move on. Living a double life, and you think it will not come back to haunt you . . . it will in due time. Karma. Don't know the answers but every day you will have a question that goes unanswered. Just a lot of thoughts going through your head, but never enough answers to the questions.

So many issues, never enough solutions . . . not enough time but a lot of discussion but never enough understanding.

—Nicole Asbury

Chapter 7

TIME

Well, time had gone by, and we were spending a lot of quality time together. I was really starting to have strong feelings for this brother, but I didn't want to get too close too soon. I was scared that I might get hurt or find out that this was a lie. You know, these days you have to be careful because some people are confused or abused by society values.

We have played around intercourse, just good-ass kissing and snuggling. I didn't know if I was ready for this brother because he was something serious to be reckoned with. Even though his job required a lot of his time, the brother would give me quality time even if just on the phone or seeing each other for just twenty minutes. This brother made time for me and didn't complain about it. He was not a punk, but I could tell this brother was very deep. It's funny how things change when you are not looking for love or anything; it just shows up. I knew I had always wanted someone to love or care for me. I would soon find out.

Chapter 8

BREAKDOWN

When Jamal touched me, my body felt like he had struck me with something unbelievable. I couldn't believe that he had a girl trying to run away from what he was trying to give to me. I was saying, slow down because this is too much. Jamal said, take my hand because I'm not going to hurt you. But Jamal still was going so fast . . . he had my mind spinning with thoughts of what was next. I couldn't explain this . . . this man was loving me like he loved money and trying to get to me like I was his money. But I couldn't, and I wasn't ready but I was . . . When I ran he ran, but then he caught up with me. He grabbed me and told me that I was his and there was no need to run because this was where I belonged—with him. I tried to get out of his arms, but his grip was tight, and he said stop fighting because he wasn't letting go. I wanted to scream, but we were so close all I could do was look at him. I was breathing hard, trying to catch my breath. I had ran so far, so long until this man caught me. I looked into his eyes. They were so warm, and I was overwhelmed with tears as he started kissing me. I couldn't resist; I wanted to, but it was no use. I invited his kiss and tongue because for once I was lost in a kiss that made me feel like I was on a cloud with the wind blowing in my hair. This man had me locked, I couldn't move. This kiss seemed like forever, but it wasn't; it was just the way it made me feel. Standing there in his arms, I felt like a marshmallow, trying to gain my composure. He looked at me and said what's wrong? I said nothing . . . and he said yes, there is. I asked him, why did he run after me?

He said, "Simple, because you are the one for me. When I wake up I can't wait to talk to you, when I see you my heart skips a beat. I get nervous when we are so close because I feel my manhood wants to stand at attention. When you speak I feel what you are saying, and I hear how you are saying it. I love the way you smell, I love the way you feel, I love the way you taste when I kiss you, I love your touch. I love that when I am with you I see it in your eyes. I love you."

Did this man just make me weaker than I was already? I couldn't believe he was loving me with all five senses. Damn, what could I say after he answered my question? He was looking at me, stroking my back with his hand, and I felt another kiss coming on. As he cradled my head in his other hand, I pulled away because I didn't want to give this man my heart and allow him to step on it.

I was saying to myself, *What am I doing? This man is confessing his love to me just like I have always wanted, and he's standing here.* I was so confused because this couldn't be happening, but it was. He came up behind me and held me, and I knew right then when he held me that everything that I was feeling was gone—all the insecurities, the confusion, and not knowing were gone. He wasn't making me do anything I didn't want to do. It was just the feeling like God said, "Be still and accept what's being given you," and I accepted it. This man was something else. I never had a man that could challenge me mentally and make me want to learn as much as I want to in the conversations we had. He would debate with me but not judge me, love me for me, and he accepted my shortcomings. When I was down, he was my support. As a couple we complement each other with everything that life has to offer. This man was mine, and I couldn't believe it, but he made me a believer.

Chapter 9

CHILLIN'

Later on that night, we cooked dinner and dined in front of the fireplace. We talked, laughed, played, and got a little tipsy, but we were together at the house chilling. The mood of the evening was filled with romance, and we danced to some smooth jazz. We decided to give each other a massage on our mats in front of the fireplace. After the massage, we fell asleep in each other's arms, warmed by the fire that burned nearby. The night was very relaxing and comforting.

Chapter 10

TRIP

We started our morning with I love you's, breakfast, and getting ready for another workday. On the drive to work, I was getting my mind ready for a staff meeting, wasn't really feeling prepared for that meeting because I had to take a trip to Paris to check out some new products that were coming out for the salon and to see my distributor. I would be out town for a week. These functions have shows and seminars. A majority of the products I use for the spa come from there. I couldn't remember if I had mentioned this to Jamal, but the trip was in a couple of days, and I had to make sure I told him.

I thought we had something planned but couldn't remember that either. The staff meeting was good, and some of the employees had some good ideas to add to the center. I was working on opening another center, but it didn't have anything to do with health, and I was working on it slowly. So it wasn't something I wanted to discuss right now. I was busy trying to get everything in order for the trip and tying up loose ends. I had a moment just thinking how special last night was and all the wonderful times together, but last night was beautiful. Jamal called and said everything I said I was thinking about last night. I said, right it was beautiful. We talked some more, and I asked him, "Do we have anything planned for this weekend?"

He said we didn't.

"Good. Because I have a business trip, and I will be gone for a week."

He was wondering, when did this come up?

"I didn't tell you?"

He said I didn't.

I said, "I'm sorry about that. I'm leaving Sunday night and will not be returning till Friday around noon."

Jamal wasn't happy, but he knew I had a business to run. He said, "I might have to take a trip with you, but I have a meeting Monday and Tuesday. I will let you know, okay?"

I was like, "Cool that would be nice if you can come." Weekend had flown by so fast, and I was getting ready to leave for Paris. Jamal asked me if I needed a ride. I told him that I was fine and that I was going to park in the parking deck. He said he was on his way to get his hug and kisses before I left. He arrived with flowers, a card, a big-ass kiss, and a hug. I told him thank you. I said I would read the card when I got on the plane. The hugs and kisses were very nice. Then I was on my way to the airport. I was kind of sad because I wished he were going with me.

Chapter 11

PARIS

I arrived in Paris, and it was so busy there. The security was really tight, and I was just glad I was able to get through with no problem. Got there and wasn't able to take in any of the nightlife or any of the Parisian famous sites. All I had time for was going to the seminars, shopping for and shipping products to the salon and spa. They had so many new things coming out for eye cellulite, reduction, and these were some of my top-selling products at the salon. I was going to some of the training classes on new things, and I was so busy during the trip. I almost forgot to call my girl. I was able to spend time with her and her family. We had dinner and talked. It was good seeing her and trying to get her to move back to the States. Being a top makeup artist kept her on the go. I was glad she was home. We said our good-byes and I love you's. I couldn't believe it was Thursday already.

On the way back to the hotel room, I decided to get some pastries. I arrived at the room, took a shower, and got ready to chow down on the pastries. There was a knock at the door, and I was like *Damn, who could that be? I don't have any clothes beside this robe.* It was room service delivering flowers from Jamal. I was so happy to see the flowers. There was a note with the flowers that said he was sorry that he wasn't able to come to Paris due to his working on a very critical deal that had to be done at the end of the week. We talked that night, and that was always good. I was really missing him. Tomorrow would be the last day, and I was leaving as soon as I could. The salon had been calling me with a problem, and I needed to get back to see what the problem was and take care of it. I took the next flight out of Paris after the last training class.

Arriving back in the States, I didn't even call Jamal when I got home because I was on the grind trying to find out what the heck was going on at the salon. It wasn't anything serious that couldn't wait till I got back. I took care of that and made a couple of phone calls. The employees wanted to know what was new—blah blah. I was tired. I told them, "I will see and talk to you guys on Monday." It was just Friday, but it was early or late. My mind was still five hours ahead and it was just 3:00 p.m. On my way home, I called Jamal, and he wanted to know what was going on. I told him I was en route to go home. He insisted that I go to his house. I said okay.

Chapter 12

WONDERFUL

I pulled into his garage, and I saw Jamal walking toward the car. I was so happy to see him because I missed him. I was getting ready to take things out of my car. He told me to leave them there. He took me by the hand and led me into the house. He told me to sit on the couch and not to move. Telling me not to move is like telling a kid, "Don't touch that candy jar."

But I sat there and waited for him to come back. I called out to him to make sure that he was okay and that he didn't forget about me. I got up and turned on some music. I was getting sleepy because of the long flight. I was a little horny but cool. I sat back down on the couch and was listening to my girl Jill Scott. I was all into one of her songs, "He Loves Me."

Then Jamal returned to where I was sitting, and I was like, "I thought you had forgot about me."

He said never. He came down the stairs with this bag. I was like, "What's in the bag?"

"Open it later, but first, I need for you to go and get into the tub."

I was like, what?

He said, "Yes, the tub. I have run you a bath. After the flight, you need to be fresh."

"Fresh."

"Just do like I ask, and you will see."

I was about to get into the tub, but I was dying to see what was in the bag. But I had to get into the garden tub. He had the bathroom lit up with candles, floating candles in the garden tub, and the music was flowing into the bathroom because this was really romantic. I undressed and laid my clothes on the side of the sink. As I was stepping into the tub, he came up behind me and slapped me on my ass.

I was like, "All right now."

He took my clothes out of the bathroom.

"What you are doing with my clothes?"

He said, "Relax and let me do this." The water was just right, not too hot or cold. The fragrance of the bubble bath was like lavender, and I love lavender, and I could feel my tired body enjoying the water. He brought me some champagne.

"Thanks for the royal treatment," I said.

He said, "You are my queen and deserve to be treated like this always." He was making me warm inside, like I wanted some of that chocolate he was toting. He's walking around in and out of the bathroom making me horny. But I had to remain cool, and I did until . . .

He came in with this dress. I was like, "Oh my goodness, you didn't." But he did. It was the dress I saw in Bloomingdale's. It was a dress that was almost lavender in color, with spaghetti straps and a split on the side. It was the kind that would fit your body in all the right places. Jamal had pulled the shoes out with the dress.

I stood in the tub, dripping water everywhere. I couldn't believe he knew what size, color, and style of shoes to get me. I was about to kiss him, but he said he was holding on because he didn't want to mess up my dress and shoes, which I would be wearing tonight.

"Okay," I said. "Thank you."

He took the dress and shoes out of the bathroom, and when he came back, he was naked.

"Oh yeah, this is what I'm taking about," he said. "You were about to jump out the tub and kiss me."

I said, "Right, I am."

He was standing there, looking so delicious and divine like a chocolate latte. I just didn't know where to start—body rippling with muscles, legs thick; his chest had hills on it that made me what to climb them. Boy, I was licking my lips, and I didn't know where to start. All I knew was that I wanted him, and I didn't care as long as he was in me. I started kissing him on his neck, then started licking his chest like there was warm caramel spread over his body. I was enjoying licking my treat.

He was starting to moan, and it was getting me hot. I started rubbing his toy with my hand. I was licking all the way down to my chocolate stick that would make me scream and come over and over . . . and it was mine. I had the chocolate stick in my hand, and I started sucking on it, and it was getting so sweet that I thought I was sucking on Tootsie Pop with that dark center. He was moaning and moving with the rhythm of my sucking on his chocolate toy. I felt the veins pulsating as I felt him getting to the point of releasing the treat that was inside. I was going faster and faster, and then he just like go of the treat. I was ready for the sweetness. He came, and I drunk my protein shake.

He looked at me and said, "Damn baby, what are you doing to me . . . trying to get a brother sprung."

I said, "No, just keeping my man satisfied."

We laughed. We got into the tub, but the water was getting cold. We ran some more water, and before you knew it, we were starting again. I was still hungry for my man, and the water was filling up the tub. I had to sit on my chocolate toy that doesn't require any batteries. I sat on the chocolate toy, and boy, it was so hard I thought it was in my throat, but it was just in my stomach. I was riding his chocolate toy. The water was going in and out of me. He cupped my ass with his hands. I was going up and down like I was on a pogo stick. He was moaning and licking my nipples. I was getting so hot.

He was like, "Damn this shit." He picked me up and took me to the bed, spread my legs and started to taste one of his favorite treats—my love canal. My legs were locked around his shoulders so I couldn't move as he was sucking on my clit, licking my love canal, and fingering me. I was having one orgasm after another.

I yelled out to him, "Suck my love canal!"

That just turned him on, and he was starting to pick up the pace, and I was getting ready to come, and boy, did I. Time for the main course, and I was ready. He put his chocolate stick gently inside me, and the pace slowed down. Because this man was making love to me, it wasn't a fuck because I knew the difference. He took his time with me. He said he could feel our hearts beating as one as we made love. Every stroke was getting deeper, and he fitted so well in my love canal. This was where he belonged. I took in a deep breath and exhaled I just feel under the spell of his lovemaking. I started getting teary-eyed because this felt so right, so good, and I was so happy.

He noticed I was starting to cry, and I said to him, "I love you too." We were getting ready to come together. I started moaning so loud, and he was right in unison with me. Then we came together. It felt like the universe had shifted. The heavy breathing had stopped, and we lay there, holding each other. We drifted off to sleep.

Later we woke up from sleep after our blissful activity earlier and decided to finally take our bath. So we could go out tonight. I was going to be looking so sexy in that the dress and shoes were on point. Damn, I hated that I didn't have the purse to go with the dress.

I asked, "Where is the bag?" It was the one that I was supposed to be open when I got out of the tub. He gave it to me. I opened the bag, and there was my lavender purse. I said, "Thank you." I jumped up on him and wrapped my legs around him, and I was kissing him, but he told me that if we didn't get out of the house, there would be another session—part 3.

I asked him if we had reservation, and he said yes. But I had the look in my eyes like I wanted part 3, just a little of it. He bent me over and took that chocolate stick and put it in my love canal from the back, and I was holding on to the dresser. I threw my leg across the top of the dress, and it was on. We were moaning together. He was looking so good in the mirror as he was tearing up my ass from the back. I came so hard that I had to go take another shower, but I was so horny that night I just wanted him, and I kept getting in trouble.

He said, "We'd never make our reservation." He got in the shower with me and picked me up as the water was hitting him on his back, and I was pinned to the wall in the shower. We were kissing each other so intensely that I could hardly kiss because he was doing some real work on my love canal. I could hardly take it.

He said, "Take it." I said, "I am taking it." His thrusts were getting harder and deeper. I was going into convulsion, my nipples were so hard, and he was kissing them. He came hard this time, and I just got that edge I was having. I felt like a child on Christmas. I was so excited. We took our shower, and this time we got dressed.

I was checking him out. I was like, *This man, this man with his fine self.* He was looking good, like one of those men in the *GQ* fashion because my man had a lot style. His hair was wavy. If he didn't cut it, it would get curly, and I loved playing with his hair. His body would make you do a double take because of that ass, those thighs, that chest, those arms, that smile, and that dick. Made a girl want to testify. I had to stop before we would really be late. We finished getting dressed. He always opened doors and closed doors for me. He was a real gentleman, not just in that way but in other ways also. He reached over and kissed me on the cheek, and I smiled. We pulled off in his Land Rover, riding to wherever this reservation was because he didn't want to tell me; it was a surprise. I was like, Cool.

Chapter 13

PARTYING

We had reservation at one of the best restaurants in Atlanta. If the food is good . . . guess what, I was there. I loved good food and desserts. Glad I had a man that loved the same and enjoyed good company. We ate and talked about the trip. We discussed what he was working on, and the love we had just made. It was off the chain! We decided not to go dancing because I was tired from the flight, and the lovemaking had drained me.

We left the restaurant, and we both were feeling the horny bug again. I was messing with him while he was driving. Thank goodness he had tinted windows. I pulled out my chocolate toy and started sucking on it while he was driving. He wasn't expecting that, but I had him going to the point that he had to pull over to get it dealt with. He couldn't believe what just happened. He said this wasn't over, and he was not going to let me get off that easy. We made it home safely. Since I was tired, we went to bed.

Chapter 14

CATCH-UP DAY

All I wanted to do was go home to unpack and just relax. I had many things to do because of the show, and we were getting ready to do a spread in one of the top massage magazines for my company. We were doing very well and were blessed to have some high-end clientele. I had to bring out the line that I got from Paris and teach the girls what I had learned. One of the company's instructors would be coming over and lecturing about this other product that I wasn't able to see because the training had been postponed. Jamal stayed in bed a little longer. I wanted to lie there with him, but I had things to do. He jumped out of the bed, remembering he had a meeting in an hour. Yes, on Saturday. I heard that money never sleeps, and the one's going to get it don't either. I drove home and got right back in bed and slept all day. I don't remember if I spoke to anyone while I was asleep or what. I knew I was tired. Jamal brought me some dinner because I wasn't going anywhere. We chilled at the house, watched a movie, and called it a night.

Chapter 15

SUNDAY

We got up and went to my church together. It was a really good sermon about keeping the faith. We chatted with some of the people in the church. We left after the service and went out for brunch. He dropped me off at my place. I told him I would get up with him later. It was football Sunday, and the fellas usually got together. I was doing my thing this Sunday. I went grocery shopping, cleaned up my house, cooked dinner, and finished balancing all my accounts. I was feeling good, and it was a beautiful Sunday.

Jamal called to see what I was doing. I could hear the guys in the background, louder than ever. I told him I was just chillin and getting ready to watch a movie. I told him that I might come over later, or I would just talk with him tonight. We exchanged I love you's and hung up. I started watching this movie on lifetime. I think I watched about thirty minutes of it before it was watching me. I didn't hear any of the phones ringing because they had fallen in between the cushions of the sofa. It was around 9:30 when he came by. I was still on the sofa asleep. He came in and tapped me on the butt, but I didn't move. He grabbed me by my shoulder to make sure I was alive.

I said, "Hey, what's going on?"

He said, "I have been calling you, and you have not answered the phone. I thought something had happened to you because the last time I talked to you was around 3:00 p.m., and now it's going on 10:00 p.m. Are you okay?"

"Yes, just tired." I told my man not to worry because I was just fine. "Just needed the rest because I have been on the go."

We went into the kitchen and ate ice cream and talked. Then all of sudden he wanted to get bad and threw the ice cream on his spoon onto my chest.

I was like, "I know you just didn't do that."

So we were in the kitchen throwing ice cream at each other. Then he grabbed me all sticky and flavored, with French vanilla running down my chest and legs. He started licking the ice cream off my chest, and I started licking the ice cream off his chest, and before we knew it, we were intertwined with each other, sticky and sweet all over.

He removed my bikini, picked me up, and placed me against the wall. He placed a leg on each shoulder and started tasting my love canal. I was trying to hold on, but there was nothing to hold on to besides his head. I was about to explode, and boy did I. He laid me down on the floor, and I all wanted to do was taste my chocolate stick because it was so creamy and sticky with the French vanilla on it, and when he was about to explode, I just put his chocolate stick into my love canal and rode it till he was calling my name and letting all his emotions go.

When he released, I just let it stay in until we fell asleep on the floor, all sticky, as we wanted to be.

I think we lay there on the floor and slept for a good while. My doorbell rang, and I was like, who was coming over and didn't call me to let me know they were coming at this time of night?

We both jumped up half naked and very sticky. "Damn, who is that?" I tried not to make a sound because I wasn't properly dressed, and nor was he. I peeped out the window to see who it was, and it was my girlfriend Tia knocking on the door like she had lost her damn mind. *Damn, girl, I'm coming*, but I had to grab a robe because I was in a sticky situation.

Jamal went and jumped into the shower where I needed to be with him. I answered the door.

"This better be important," I told Tia.

She said she needed something to drink because she was stressed out.

I said, "What's going on now that you couldn't call me?"

She said she did but I never answered either phone.

I told her, "My bad, they fell in between the sofa cushions." I never did get the remotes or the phones out when Jamal came over. I felt for them but never retrieved them. I said, "What's up with you, then?"

She was stressing over her man as usual, and she thought he was just trifling, but she loved him.

"If love makes you stressed, please keep it away from me."

She went into the kitchen, but she turned back around and said, "You and Jamal are so nasty."

"What are you talking about?"

"Because there is ice cream all over the floor, and I can tell you had him and a little party right on the floor."

I said, "Girl, stop." She started to interrupt me, and I said no, because we were asleep.

She said, "I bet." She just wanted to vent her frustration out. Jamal came back up front to clean up our mess.

"What's going on, Tia?" he asked.

"Nothing, but I'm getting ready to go."

She left, and I was heading to the bathroom to take off these sticky clothes. Then Jamal said, "We are not finished."

"Oh yes, we are."

He went into the kitchen to clean the mess. I ran to the bathroom because I knew he would try me in the shower and out. I was trying to catch up on the nap earlier. But it was no use when I got out of the shower. He was looking at me, waiting to dry me off. He took the towel and wrapped part of my body with it. And then he sat on the toilet and pulled me near and started licking me dry. He was kissing my stomach, sucking on my breast, getting all the water off every body part. Just him licking and kissing me. I think I got two orgasms just by his touch. He picked me up and looked into my eyes and said, "I love you, Sparkle." I said, "I love you, too."

Jamal put me on the bed, and we fell asleep in each other's arms.

Chapter 16

You

Even though it was a Monday morning, last night was just lovely. I couldn't even complain. I went into the kitchen. The kitchen was clean from last night, and he was cooking some breakfast. I started feeling the poetic side of me wanting to come out as I started thinking about how this man made me feel.

Poetic—moment—you

I see you standing there, and all I can say is what a man. Thoughts go through my head when I try to say what I am feeling. I get speechless. When you smile you light up my inner emotions. When you look at me it's like you have undressed me with your eyes. Your touch makes me quiver; it makes me long for you. When you take me into your arms I feel protected and comfortable, like this is where I belong. Your arms suppress all the chaos from a hard day. As you speak, I hold on to every word. Your lips are so irresistible that I could just kiss and suck on them.

He turned around and said, "What are you thinking?"

I said, "You." He had cooked a big breakfast. We sat there, eating, talking, and then cleaning up the kitchen. He said he had to go into the office and take care of some things. We both got dressed and left to go to work.

I had to take care of the products from Paris and see if I had any clients for this week. I knew I had to schedule a training class for these products and take inventory. Well, I was very busy at the spa, taking care of any issues and mailers that had to go out. Mother's Day was right around the corner. I needed to get gift certificates ready and make sure that the mailers got out on time. The spa gets really busy this time of the year, and I had to make schedules and cut checks for accounting. Throughout the day, we talked or just called to say we were thinking about each other.

I left the spa around 7:00 p.m., and Jamal left his office around 5:30 p.m. He was starting to get worried, so I said I would be home soon. He said he was going out with the fellas. I was cool with him going because I was tired, and I needed some sleep. My man had me singing in the opera for the past two days. All I wanted to do was go to bed (and actually sleep). He said he would probably spend the night after he finished hanging out with the fellas.

The girls were calling to see if I wanted to go out to eat. I told them I needed my rest, and besides I couldn't hang out with them all because I wouldn't be able to get up in the morning. I said, "Let's make a date for this Friday to go out to eat." And we all agreed. I went home and took a long hot bath and just reflected on what had happened in the last four months. I got into bed wearing only a silk gown. I needed my sweet kitten to breathe, and I needed sleep. I was sleeping so good I didn't hear him come in.

Jamal kissed me on my shoulder and just stood looking down at me. I asked him, "Why are you staring at me while I'm asleep?"

He said, "You look so peaceful."

I said okay and that I was going right back to sleep. He pulled the covers off me.

My gown was wrapped around me, and my shaven cat was uncovered, and he must have thought she was purring back at him because he smiled and said, "Ahh, there goes my friendly pussycat."

I pulled the covers back on and fixed my gown right.

He said, "I know you are not trying to hide from me."

"No, but I'm tired, baby."

Jamal repeated, "I know you are not trying to hold out of me. You know I haven't had my love medicine for today."

"You had an overdose yesterday and last night."

"I'm here now because night has arrived again, and I'm ready for your kitten. That's why I didn't bother you this morning because I knew you needed your sleep. I thought, *This man had worn this girl out, and she needs some rest*."

I said, "Go take a cold shower, you will feel better, and it will calm you down from being horny.

He took his shower and afterward got into bed. He immediately started kissing my back and rubbing my breasts. I grabbed his hands and just held on to them, and before you knew it, he was sleep. I said, "Thank you, Jesus."

I went right back to sleep. I woke up earlier, and since my man thought I was holding out on him, I thought I would give him a treat.

Chapter 17

A WAKE-UP CALL

He was sleeping on his back—so peaceful that he didn't hear me stir around in the bed. I started rubbing my thunder underneath the covers. Since my man sleeps nude majority of the time, it was easy for me take the opportunity to do what I liked to do—please my man. I started stroking him, slowly moving up and down with my hand wrapped around his thunder. I knew he knew I was messing with it, but he didn't know I was getting ready to taste the thunder. While I was putting it down on him, he started rubbing my ass and fingering me. Because I was already turned on from giving him head and the moans he made excited me, I was so wet that he was saying "Damn, baby" while I was still sucking on him. He was trying to get me to stop because he wanted to enter, but I would not let up on it. I was deep-throating, and before long, he was coming.

That morning was all about him being served, and I served him so well that he went right back to sleep after I got my supplement. By the time he rose, I was already at work and had left him in bed. He called me and said he felt like Eddie Murphy in *Boomerang*. The only thing I didn't do was leave the money on the stand. I started laughing, and I told him to have a wonderful day. We exchanged I love you's and hung up the phone.

Chapter 18

HANGING OUT WITH THE GIRLS

This week went by so fast. But I was glad it was the end of the week. My girls had been calling me all week, asking if we were still on for tonight. I told them we were still on and wanted to know where we were going. They wanted to have dinner and go dancing. We went to the Atlanta Fish Market, an upscale seafood restaurant, and then went out dancing. We talked about everything. It was wonderful having my girls around. We were all in relationships, and though we might flirt, we never crossed the line. That's what we girls do when we're out having fun and getting our laugh on and our dance on. Our mates had called us to see if we were all right and so forth. You know men; they have to make sure that no one is trying to step in the back door. It's funny, but that's how men sometimes show their affection.

The night was a blast, and I think we were all tipsy but cool enough to drive. We gave each other hugs and kisses and called it a night. On the way home, I called Jamal to see if he was up or out himself. He was home and up working on another deal that he was trying to finalize by Monday. I asked him if he was hungry. He said yes. He told me to come over and we would cook something when I get there.

I said cool and planned to be there in fifteen minutes. I arrived at Jamal's, and he gave me a hug and a kiss. "Talking about did you wear that out?"

I said, "Don't act, it was just a dress, but it was a dress that showed my assets."

He smacked me on the ass and said, "It's all good. I'm looking in the fridge trying to find us something to eat. I could eat breakfast all day."

I asked him if he wanted some breakfast, and he said no. "A sandwhich." He said no.

"What then?" I asked

"You!"

I just looked at him, and he had the hungry look like he could tear my ass up. He was standing behind me as I bent over the fridge, and I felt him pressing against me. He pulled me to him, and he kissed me so intensely that my nipples started getting hard. He put me on the counter, and the fridge was still open. He removed my G-string with his teeth. He placed my left leg on his right shoulder and started licking inside my inner thigh. Then he placed my right leg on his left shoulder and did the same with my right inner thigh. I could feel myself getting wet, and he looked at me. I didn't know what he had in his hands.

It was chocolate sauce, and he poured it on my bunny. The feeling of the sauce was cool and sticky, but that was all right because it was making me wetter. I quickly pulled off my dress. I didn't want to get sticky sauce on it. He was sucking, licking my bunny like he hadn't eaten in days. He was gentle but intense. He grabbed some grapes, pineapple slices, mandarin orange slices, and what other fruits. He placed some of the fruit inside my love canal and started eating it out. When I was coming, he made each orgasm stronger than the other. I was trying to get my balance on the counter and was stretched out with fruit and chocolate sauce all over me.

Jamal was licking and sucking on every part of me. He didn't leave a spot untouched. I felt like I had hit the jackpot and won the biggest lottery ever. I can't count how many times I came, but I know I was weak. I was telling Jamal that I had to give him props for his tongue because that was a deadly weapon.

I was about to get up, and he said, "Where are you going?"

I said, "Nowhere."

Jamal pulled me up to him and slid his magic wand in me. He whispered in my ear, telling me that he loved me, I was his queen, and I would always be. I told him that I loved him and he was my king always.

We were making love right there on the countertop. The lovemaking was off the hook. We took our shower and went to sleep in each other's arms. I slept like a baby. The next morning, thank God, was a Saturday, because after all this sexing, I needed to sleep, but I had a busy day.

I noticed that Jamal wasn't in bed. I got up and went into the kitchen. I was hungry because I didn't eat anything last night, and I was starving. Jamal had toasted some bagels, and I told him I had to hurry out the door because I had some things to take care of. Jamal fixed my bagel, gave me bottled water, and kissed me. I told him I would call him in a few.

On the way to the office, Jamal called me on the phone and asked if I'd be ready tonight around 7:00 p.m. because we had a reservation. I told him yes, I would be ready. I stayed in the office for about four hours. I got home in time to get ready for the date.

Jamal picked me up at 7:00 p.m. We chatted about our day, and I wanted to know where we were going, but it was a surprise.

Chapter 19

ENGAGEMENT

We arrived at this restaurant I'd heard about that had really good food. Anything that had good food I was down for as long as it served chicken, turkey, and seafood. The restaurant decor created a very pleasant atmosphere, and you could smell the tasty aromas from the kitchen. I was definitely feeling this place. I could see it had its own old-school jazz band, and I love some good jazz. Some of the people where bobbing their head and tapping their feet to the music. Some even got up and danced. It was lovely. He told me it took awhile to get on the reservation list because it was new and because of what it was presenting—live jazz, good food, and a nice atmosphere. We were seated at our table, but this table wasn't for two people, nor was it decorated like the rest.

I was like, "Why are we sitting at this big table?"

Jamal said this was the only table they had and he didn't know why they decorated like this. I felt like something was getting ready to go down, but I was like, "Okay." We ordered some chardonnay, and the taste was excellent. Then I saw some of my girlfriends with their boyfriends or husbands and some of his friends with their ladies. My girlfriends complimented me on my outfit, and I said thanks. They came to sit at the table. Everyone was mingling and getting acquainted with each other at the table.

Jamal looked around to make sure that everyone was at the table. Then the waiter came and poured everyone a glass of champagne. I looked at Jamal with a raised eyebrow, wondering, *What's going on?* Then Jamal decided to get up and make a toast. The jazz band was in tune with what he was saying as he thanked everyone for coming and announced that he had something to say.

I was looking at him while he spoke about me. He said, "This woman right here that's seated in front of me is my queen and my world. She's my everything."

I was starting to blush, and then he said, "I love Sparkle with my entire heart. I feel the love she gives me, I hear the sound of our hearts beating as one when we are together. I love the way she smells, I see the love in her eyes." To me he said, "I love you."

He got down on his knee, pulled out this blue tiffany box, opened it, and asked me to marry him. I almost couldn't control the tears that were flowing down my cheek. He took the ring out of the box, and I said yes, and he put the ring on my finger. We kissed so passionately that my girlfriends were like, *Okay that's enough.*

I heard a two very familiar voice say "Congratulations" from the background. It was my parents! They were sitting far on the other side. This was another surprise. He had planned this for a while. I was so happy. Everyone ordered food and drinks, and it was wonderful. We were dancing, laughing, sharing stories, and just having a wonderful time. But I was in another world. I was so happy and content with this man.

He grabbed my hand and kissed the inside of my palm, and I rubbed his face with my hand. He gave me that look and whispered in my ear, "You are mine."

We were alone for a couple minutes, and we were getting in the mood for some lovemaking. He whispered in my ear and said he couldn't wait to be my husband. I blushed to myself and my hand went under the table into his lap and rubbed his scrotum. I was almost caught by Mom, of all people. She was getting ready to say something, and all she could do was smile. I smiled back.

Jamal whispered in my ear and said, "Hot ass."

I giggled to myself. I smiled back. We just laughed at each other because I was caught. I got up and spoke with my mom. She was so happy for me, and she knew that a special someone would find me, and he did. I told my mom that I loved him with all my heart, and she said, "I know, baby and he loves you very deeply too."

Then my father came, and he was congratulating us, and he was happy also. My father and my mother left me to dance. Jamal said it was our time to dance.

I said, "Okay, Mr. Princeton. Would you like to dance with the future Mrs. Princeton? He said yes.

The jazz band started to play some slow music that sounded like K-Ci and JoJo's "All My Life." I was feeling that joint and him also. We danced, and he was holding me so tight that I could feel everything. We lost ourselves in each other. He was looking into my eyes and started kissing me. We were kissing, and it felt like the room was spinning around us because we were vibing with each other. Our friends came onto the floor and started dancing. We came back and started having fun all over again. That was a wonderful night. I can see why it takes a long time to get on the reservation list.

After the surprise engagement, everyone went their separate ways. I told my parents thanks for coming and that I loved them. They were congratulating Jamal and welcoming him to the family. Being welcome to the family made him feel good. I hated that his parents were not able to come due to the bad weather but they congratulated me and welcomed me to their family. Both of the parents got along so well and stated they were still coming when they could get a flight out the next day because they were losing power, and the flights were being cancelled. We said would see them when they got here and told them to try to stay warm.

Chapter 20

PLANNING OR NOT?

The next couple weeks were hectic for both of us. We hadn't really been able to spend much quality time together as we usually did. I had to start planning this wedding because we hadn't had time to discuss, or I just hadn't had time to think about it. I was engaged and not talking about a wedding was unrealistic because this was something that I had always wanted, and now I got my king. I would take care of the wedding date and the planning with Jamal when I got the chance. And that was all the time I had. I was just so engulf in him about other things. He asked and even told me the date he wanted to get married on and everything, but I heard but didn't listen. Off to work because the spa sometimes seemed as though it couldn't work without me.

I went in, and I had a client to meet, but I never met this guy before. He had already done the paperwork and it was lying on the table. I went and introduce myself and asked what his concerns were for his massage and what type since this was his first time. I had turned my back on him to hang the clipboard back on the wall. As I was getting ready to start the massage, I noticed something very similar. When I pulled the covers back, he grabbed me, and before I knew it he had started kissing me, and it was Jamal. I was like, "I know you didn't come in here to get a massage."

He said, "Yes, I thought this will surprise you."

"Yes, it did. So do you want a massage? See, I scheduled once but never came back because we ended up dating, then I decided that since you will be my wife, why not come back down and pick up were I left off?"

He wanted a massage, but he wanted the type you would get in the Oriental spas. I was like, "You know I don't do that." But what the hell, he paid for the session, and this was my man. I had to lock the door because I didn't want anyone coming in or disturbing his one-hour session. He lay prone on the table, and I massaged his back, legs, and before you knew it, he was sleep. I told him to turn over so I could work on his front. He grabbed me, and I was on top, and his manhood was so hard that I couldn't resist the urge to please him. I pleased him, and when I did that, he wanted to please me, but I was like, "You know, time is about up."

But he wanted me bent over the table, and I obliged him. That was awesome session. He got dressed, and the girls up front were smiling and looking to see if I had a smile or glow going on. I was acting like nothing happened, but it did. He paid for the session and gave me a tip and a note.

Jamal wanted me to meet him at the Westin Hotel Sundial tonight at seven because we needed to talk. I had four clients to do. The rest of the day went by so fast, but I needed that charge of energy from my man. I wanted to know what he had to talk to me about. Finished with my clients and so with the paperwork, I was out of the office around 4:00 p.m. He called me to see if I would be there tonight, or I wanted him to pick me up. I said I would meet him there because sometimes I take longer than usual to get dressed.

That's why he asked to come and pick me up. I rode by the Fox Theater and saw that they had one of Tyler Perry's plays coming to town. I was like, *I need to check that out because we haven't been to any plays in a while or to a neo soul concerts. That will be one of the things I will add to the conversation tonight.* I forgot I had to take care of so many things at the rental property. I was like, *I would be pushing it tonight because it is already 5:00 p.m.* I took care of the issues, and it was a quarter to six when I was finished. I had to hurry up. I didn't know what to wear. I pulled out my blue silhouette dress with the splits on the side that went past my knees. It was an attention grabber, but that was the whole point. I pulled out my heels that went with the dress and the purse. I jumped into the shower, and the phone was ringing. I'm glad I had the cordless in the bathroom. It was Jamal saying he was coming to get me because he knew I would be late. I said okay. I finished taking the shower, lotioned up, perfumed up, and dressed up. I had my hair up. So it didn't really need too much done to it. Thank God for hairstylists. It was about 6:45 p.m., and he walked in.

"Are you ready?"

I said, "Yes, just let me get my purse, lip liner, gloss, and little eye shadow, and I will be ready."

It was 7:00 p.m. when we left. He told me that I looked good and that I was wearing the hell out of the dress. He told me that our reservation was at 7:30 p.m., and I said, "I thought you said 7:00 p.m. I told you that so you would have your behind ready. I have to change times on you because you forget about time. You with your colored-people time zone."

I started laughing. "You think you know huh?

He said, "I'm learning."

We arrived at the Sundial on time. We ordered our drinks. Then he started talking about our wedding and the date. He wanted to know if I had decided on a date.

I said, "To be honest with you, I haven't thought of a date, but I'm open to any suggestion or comparison."

He stated that he wanted to get married in June. I was like, "Next year."

He said, "This year."

I was like, "It's already March."

"I know because we have been engaged for two months, Sparkle, and we haven't set a date or something."

"Baby, that is so close."

He said, "I can't wait to be your husband, and I don't know why it's taking you so long to decide if you want to be my wife."

"What are talking about? I just haven't thought about the date."

"When do you want to get married?"

I was like, "Hurry up with the drinks." He was getting over me with this conversation. I didn't have a problem with marrying; it was just that I didn't know if I was ready that soon. He asked if I wanted to get married at the justice of peace. I was like no.

He asked, "What is the date?"

"The first Saturday in June."

"If money is a problem, you know I got you."

"It's not the money. Just got to get everyone together and spring the date on them and see if they can participate in the wedding."

He asked me if I wanted a big wedding, and I was like, "No, I don't need twelve bridesmaids. I would probably have five bridesmaids.

He was like, "Cool, that isn't bad.

I said I already had some ideas and that I had picked out my dress for the wedding and just had to go and get fitted for it.

He said, "Just go with the ideas."

Chapter 21

THINKING

I didn't know what to say or think anymore. Could I be moving too fast, or did he really know what he wanted? So many questions, and I thought I needed to ask him these questions. Because I just felt like there were things missing. Before I'd marry anyone, it had to be right. I didn't want to end up with an annulment or a divorce in two or three years. I just couldn't do it if love wasn't the main factor. This would have to be forever.

Chapter 22

UNCERTAINTY

Things between us had been great, but certain things were starting to stick out. I had been paying attention to the phone calls ranging from being short too not many at all, quality-time slacking and just being able to take a trip. I didn't know if I was having cold feet, or if I was I looking for a way out. I just didn't know what to think right now. Jamal's behavior had been totally different, like something was bothering him. He said it was nothing, but I knew it was something.

Chapter 23

SURPRISE

That night I came over to his house, but I didn't park in the garage. He was playing loud music, something that he didn't do. I mean, he played it, but not to the extreme. He didn't hear me come in, and I noticed he was on the phone talking to someone. Whoever the person was, he was getting very upset with. I tried to sneak up or let him know I was there. Whomever he was talking to, he was really letting that person have it. I knew it wasn't a dude because he used words I never heard him speak. I didn't know what to do, whether I should say something or just walk back out the door and reenter. He was walking upstairs into his bedroom, and I could really hear the conversation then. He was telling the person, "It's over. Don't call me no more."

I was saying to myself, *What the fuck is going on?"* I was trying to hold my composure because I was ready to go upside his head. Then I heard the doorbell ring, and I was like, *Who in the world's at the door?* I didn't park in the garage, and number two, he would know I was in the house. I was like, *What do I do?* I had to think fast; I ran downstairs to the half bath and pretended that I used the bathroom. So when he came downstairs, I was coming out the bathroom.

He said, "Was that you ringing the bell?"

I was like, "No, I was in the bathroom." He had the phone in his hand still, and I wanted to know who was at the door and who in the hell was on the phone. The doorbell was ringing like crazy.

I said, "Do you want me to get it?"

He said he would, but I was right behind him because I needed to know who it was ringing my fiancé's door like that. We both get to the door, remind you the phone was still in his hands. I wanted the phone, but when he opened the damn door, there was a damn woman at the door running her mouth, and I was like, "What the hell is going on?"

She said she had been kicking it with my man for the past month, and she wanted to know what was going on with him, and why wasn't he answering the phone and so forth? I looked at him, and the phone in his hand before I could say anything.

This bitch pushed herself into the house, and he was trying to get her out and in the process the phone fell out of his hand. I picked up the phone and turned the Mute off and said hello.

She was like, "Who is this?"

I said, "First of all, you are on my fiancé's phone. Who are you?"

She said that she was his woman and that they started talking about two weeks ago. I was like, what the fuck? Before I knew it, I was in full kick-your-ass mode. I grabbed him by the back of his neck and asked him, "What's going on?"

This bitch was still running her damn mouth, and I told her to shut the fuck up before I stick my damn fist down her throat.

To Jamal I said, "And sit down somewhere because we are going to get to the bottom of this." And I told the chick on the phone to bring her ass over, she already knew the address. When she arrived, I was about two seconds from stabbing his ass, but I wasn't going to jail for no one. She arrived, and these women were women, how could you say crazy? I know I might sound crazy, but nowhere near this bullshit. One of these women he used to kick it with before we got involved, and he stated that it was over between them. She was still calling, and he was calling too. So she said she was pregnant by him.

I was like, "What did you just say?"

She said she was pregnant and it was his.

I was like, *One-two-three* and went upside his head with my fist, and he grabbed me, telling me she was lying.

I said, "Get your motherfucking hands off me. Step away before I cut the shit out of you." Those heifers were looking like that bitch was crazy. I was the crazy one that night. I asked the other heifer what was her reason for blowing up his phone like she was crazy. She said that he has being paying for sex from her, and she had developed feelings, and she wanted more. I was getting ready to go outside and put a cap in his ass. He wouldn't let me go outside 'cause he knew what was going down.

I said, "You are paying for sex?" I asked her her name. She said Sandra. She was a call girl, and she didn't live here. "When he goes on a business trip, I usually accompany him." I was like, "Whoa. When do you accompany him? I'm mostly there."

She said, "I have only done it twice."

I was like, "When were these times?" The first time we weren't involved, and the second time one week before he met me, so I was cool with that part. She said that she wanted him, and she wasn't leaving there without him. I told her to get a life and stop falling in love with the dick.

Sandra said he told her that he might pursue a relationship with her. "But that's when he met you, and he stopped communicating with me, and I was hurt. I never heard from him until a week ago. Telling me he was sorry and all this stuff. I was still in love with him because I wanted everything about him. So that's why I was blowing up his phone. He called me and stated that he was sorry. So I want what I want, and that's Jamal."

"He called you to make amends with you, not get with you." Now Jamal hadn't opened his mouth at all. I was looking at him for his reasoning or whatever, but nothing came out of his mouth. Nothing. The girl that was pregnant was Violet, and she said she never stopped messing around with him. Next thing I knew it, I woke up on the floor with an African stick in my hand. I must have blacked out or something. I looked around and saw Jamal on the floor, bleeding. Violet and Sandra both were gone. I couldn't remember shit. I got up and went over to Jamal to see if he was okay, but I was thinking to myself, *How in the world did I end up with the stick in my hand? Put two and two together, those bitches must have been working together.*

I called out to Jamal, but he didn't answer. A girl was not going to jail for no bullshit. I had too much to lose for some nonsense. Jamal started moving around on the floor, saying his head hurt. I asked him what happened, and he said he couldn't remember completely what happened. He just knew that we both were in a deep argument and those women were looking, and he noticed that Violet had picked up his African stick and "before you could turn around she hit you and then me; so that heifer is trying to set this mess up with you and me." We heard the police sirens, and then someone was knocking at the door. I was like, *Damn what are we going to do?*

I grabbed the stick and wiped down where my hands were and put it in the corner. The police came in said that they got a call about domestic violence, and we said we were fine. The officer stated that they needed to view the premises before he left. On the floor was the blood; Jamal was still bleeding, but he was trying to cover it up. He couldn't because it was trickling down the back of his neck. I was like, *Damn. This isn't looking good.*

The officer said, "Would you like to place charges against her?"

Jamal said no, and before he could say anything, he passed out. Guess what, I would go to jail for domestic violence. Jamal was in the hospital a unconscious and with stitches.

I was so pissed off about this shit. I called my girl to come and get me out of jail. She arrived and couldn't believe the bullshit. When I got out of jail, I saw I had like ten missed calls from the same number. I was like, *Who is this and why are they calling like this?* Before I could check my voice mail, the phone rang. I said hello, and the person on the other end said, "I got you, bitch."

I was like, "What?"

"I know your secrets, and I know you been to jail, and I will make you burn if you don't leave Jamal alone. I will contact you again and you better walk away from him." Then she hung up. The number was from a pay phone. So who in the world could this be now? I could only think of one of those two heifers at the house.

To be continued . . .

EPILOGUE

Well, what can I say? When you think you have found true love that feels real, you find it was just a fragment of your imagination. Sparkle had realized that all the men she had dated or been with always came back in some way. But she was tired of the men that played, used, and abused her because she was done with all the heartache and the lies that were told to her. It was time to live again, time to enjoy love no matter how things might be going. It was time to be let go and be happy. She thought Jamal was her prince, but she realized that he was like the rest, just someone that had issues that came back to haunt them, someone that didn't want to work together to resolve them, and I felt it was time for a new beginning. Have you ever wondered when a change will come? And when it does come, are you willing to accept the change in your life? It's time for a change for me. I have gone through some many things; who would have ever wondered if I could have found happiness? And I know happiness comes from within. I can't believe all the time and effort needed to make it work, and then all I get is the hurt and the one holding the stick. But no more, because a change was going to come. Mr. Princeton taught me a lot even though things changed drastically, but he did give me the love and understanding to be able to open my heart again. I know love exist, and I thank him for sharing his love and not making me bitter. I know when the next man that comes into my life I will be ready. I know what I want and how I want to be treated. Sometimes you think you have that prince, but sometimes that prince has secrets that can take him through some challenges, but if he has a woman that is holding on and carrying him when he is down, why does he turn his back on what they have built together, or trying to build together?

Chances

Chances are free

Chances are choices but it's up to you if you want to take that chance

Do you want the chance to love?

Do you want the chance for love to love you?

Are you ready for that chance?

Can you tell me if this is something you're ready for?

Are you ready for the chance that can make you or break you?